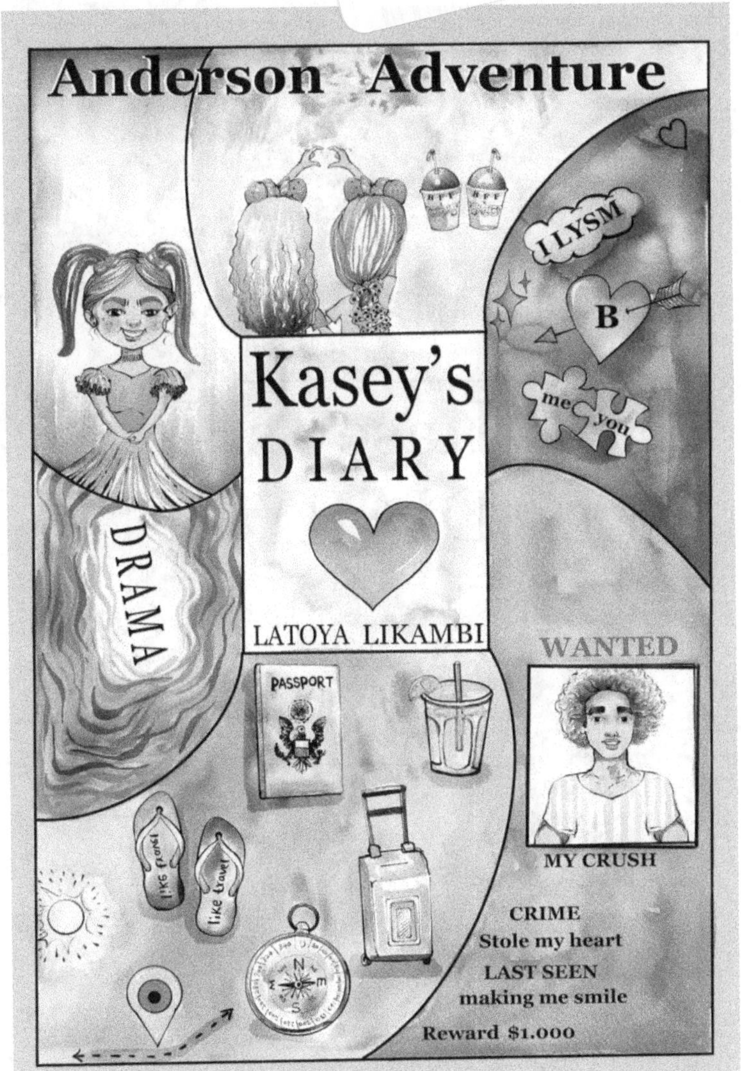
Anderson Adventure
ILYSM
B
me
you
Kasey's
DIARY
LATOYA LIKAMBI
DRAMA
PASSPORT
WANTED
MY CRUSH
like travel
like travel
CRIME
Stole my heart
LAST SEEN
making me smile
Reward $1.000

the Anderson family!!!
POPULAR
14ᵗʰ
Kasey's
DIARY
LATOYA LIKAMBI
LONDON
AVA + EVA
= DOUBLE TROUBLE
ABC 123
School
NEW TEACHER
00:03
12
1
2
3
4
5
6
7
8
9
10
11

Kasey's Diary

Anderson Adventure

Latoya Likambi

First published in Great Britain in 2020 by Likambi Global Publishing

www.likambiglobalpublishing.com

ISBN-13:978-1-913266-99-8

Many Thanks

Thanks to everyone for buying my book! However, there are some specific people I would like to particularly thank. Keira (my amazing cousin), thanks so much for showing love for my books; Kirsten and Aiyven, I wish you the best of luck with your books and your YouTube channel and many wishes of success to you! Last but not least, I would like to give a HUGE thank you to all my internet siblings from my YouTube channel. My siblings (Caleb and Destiny) and I love you guys a bunch; thanks for supporting us, if it weren't for you all, we wouldn't have been putting effort into the content we create on YouTube. Now, let's get on to the best part (the actual diary, LOL) ☺.

CONTENTS

CHAPTER 1:

My Birthday Bash

OMG, my party in December was a huge success! It was ... awesome, I'm dying to write about it all! However, right now I'm so annoyed with Mom and Dad, but I'll save that story for later. ☹ Now, back to my party and, yes, it was actually (almost) drama-free! ☺

First of all, my crush Blake came and gave me the cutest gift ever, which was a ... PUPPY! I never in a million years thought he would ever take into consideration that I've always wanted one and I definitely didn't think he would go out of his way to somehow get enough money for a puppy, FOR ME!

Also, my family, guests, BFFs, and I had such a great time dancing, singing, laughing, and exchanging funny stories.

I was also super glad and grateful that all the guests made it safely and brought me SO MANY PRESENTS! OMG, the pile of gifts I received was unbelievably tall and might have even been tall enough to reach the sun (okay,

maybe I overreacted there, LOL).

My usually CRAZY family was actually acting more 'normal' than usual

and Lilly actually managed to stay composed.

Well ... she was composed until she DROPED MY DAMN CAKE ON THE FLOOR! ☹ But guess what; I had a BACKUP cake! Like seriously, my family would never have saved up extra money to buy ME a backup cake. I was so shocked that I wondered were my parents THAT thoughtful? It was as if they actually THOUGHT of me before Lilly for once.

Anyway, for one of my last presents I got... A new phone that was actually good! OMG, my heart jumped out of my chest to the MOON and back when I opened this gift. I could immediately guess who had bought me this gift. It was from Nana Gracie because she has always had good taste and an expensive lifestyle and has such a "rich" mentality. She earned TONS of money from her business! If she isn't styling hair, she spends her time vintage shopping and spoiling her pretty dog Diamond. Diamond is her Pomeranian dog. I don't think Diamond particularly likes me though. I am personally informing you that, yes, Diamond may look cute, but she is deceptive and has her beady little eyes scanning me all the time! Honestly, I think Nana pampers her too much. They cruise together and she has her very own designer dog lead. Likeeee OMG, I wish I got the same treatment as her.

Anyway, I felt very proud because I had been asking—no—BEGGING for a new phone because my old one was a crusty dusty hand-me-down and literally never had any storage left. Lily always took it to play games and she would return it to me with like a thousand cracks on the screen. ☹

Now I have the new iPhone! I had finally pushed the fact into my parents' face that I WAS responsible enough for a proper phone that wasn't some used, cracked-up thing.

I could tell Mom was very annoyed just by her expression. Even though she tried to look calm, I could feel her blazing hazel eyes piercing through me, OUCH! She even tried to talk Nana Gracie into taking back the phone when the party was over. I was so mad with Mom and embarrassed! She was like, "Kasey has a perfectly fine phone," and, "You can spend that money on Diamond instead." Excuse me Mom? Diamond already has enough expensive things.

Luckily for us, whenever Lilly and I visited Nana (which was often) I always complained and whinged to her about how bad my phone was, and Nana believes that kids these days should have access to better technology. Therefore, it was a no-brainer and Mom can't do anything about it—HA!

Today, I headed over to social studies in a very good vibe to work on my assigned project with Gloria and Rebecca (my partners). As usual, we were multitasking (talking and working). A few minutes after the lesson started, when I looked over at the table beside us (Brittany's table), the girls were taking selfies on Brit's phone!

Just looking at their crusty little pouts annoyed me so much and they sure knew by now that we were forbidden to use phones in the classroom. I snarled at them, sickeningly pouting their dry lips at the phone, and nudged Gloria to look over.

Unfortunately, Gloria made a loud remark and whisper-shouted, "Ugh, seriously? Taking selfies on their phone in class!"

Brittney looked over, snarled at us and quickly hid her phone in her purse. Then Eliza went ahead and said, "You do know we were just looking at our calculator!" We shrugged and turned back around again…

Although, in our heads, we all knew that only a slow person would believe THAT! Come on, we're not stupid:

1. You don't need a calculator in social studies

2. Who pouts at a calculator?

And if it were a calculator, why would you need to hide it?

I really don't know what stupid game they were trying to play, but it wasn't working at all.

Then the bell rang and I did the biggest eye roll I could before dragging myself up to trudge over to the next lesson, which was swimming class (aka my worst subject).

As we made our way to the lesson, Brittany was talking with some girl (I'm guessing she's new). She was a pretty girl, very tall, and looked like a darker version of Brittany.

This girl had the shiniest, kinkiest, brunette locks I had ever seen! They bounced in rhythm as she walked as if she was a model on a runway.

Let me tell you something, I have been here for hundreds—no—THOUSANDS of years (okay, I got carried away). STILL, I've attended this school for a long time and no one pays attention to me except my friends and the tutors! However, THIS new girl was getting the attention of the WHOLE school by simply being present. Word spread in less than two seconds and, apparently, the new girl was called Keira and was Brittany's new younger cousin from Barcelona, Spain.

My face cringed and my stomach flipped. Oh great! This meant that I had to deal with another wannabe Brittany for almost THE REST OF MY LIFE! Gloria, Rebecca, and I sighed in unison, knowing what was about to become of this school. ☹

Keira turned around and pointed at me with a confused expression. My pulse increased immediately; I hadn't even met this girl yet and Brittany was probably giving her bad impression of me already...

Keira stood up and walked towards me, I was so nervous I felt like running far away until I got to my bedroom. I was about to pretend to look for something in my purse then I realised I HADN'T brought it! Too late now, I looked like a complete fool. Instead, I just stood there as she looked me up and down curiously. When I finally came to my senses, I blurted, "Hey! I'm Kasey, it's probably hard to believe, but any rumours you've heard about me were fake. I promise I'm not as scandalous as you might think I am."

Instead of insulting me, she said, "Hi! It's fine, I could see you're nervous from your eyes ... you probably thought I was coming over to accuse you of something. I'm actually not like my cousin Brit at all; I know she can be a pain in the backside."

I chuckled. "Well, you can say that again!" I said, clasping my mouth with my hand afterwards in case Brittany heard.

She continued, "In fact, we're so different... We're usually fighting all the time and she's always getting on my nerves. Anyway, I was wondering if you would like to be my study partner, since I need some new friends." My nerves disappeared instantly and my face glowed; so she WASN'T coming to insult me OR accuse me of anything! ☺

Before I jumped up and said yes, I had to excuse myself to ask my former study partner if I could work with Keira—just for the day. Luckily, he was cool with it (it was Jayden anyway and he was a chill person in general).

***

The week went by quickly and we all had a blast with Keira. She taught me cool tricks in dodge ball, she included me AND my BFFs in every conversation and she even taught us how to bribe the teachers into letting us out of lessons 10 minutes earlier with a fake lunch pass and a small box of chocolates. We also taught her a few things, like how to get a free lunch meal, and we showed her our secret archive up in the library.☺

Each day, after school, we always stopped at the ice bar and would get the mango flake popsicles; I savored the cold, sweet flavor on the tip of my tongue as we walked in unison and talked until we got home... Our first two weeks with Keira were the best! Life seemed perfect and I longed for it to stay that way.

I'm really looking forward to hanging out with my BSFs and Keira tomorrow at the mall.

***

Back home there was a huge DINNER DISASTER! Ugh, this is so gross that I can't even write about it without gagging! Basically, Dad still believes in all women doing a bunch of domestic work and all that olden-day stuff. So today, Dad decides that seven-year-old Lilly (who can't even make toast without burning it) needs to learn to cook because she will be a "big girl" soon.

So she had to help him make dinner. I was genuinely very afraid of what would happen in the kitchen, so I decided to pretend to feel sick and have a case of "severe constipation". Even though I was just locked up in my en suite scrolling through my Instagram feed, my parents thought I was really constipated, so my plan was working so far ☺. Soon after, a terrible pungent smell infested my nostrils! The fumes were so stinky they were probably DEADLY! I hid my head in my knees and dug my face deeper into my knees, thinking it would help. Err, NO! These stinkin' fumes squeezed through all the cracks in the room and attacked my fragile nose.☺

Just as I thought things were calming down, tendrils of smoke filled the air and suffocated my lungs. I was coughing, retching, and struggling to get out of my en suite. When I finally did, my bedroom door was locked. I'm guessing Lilly ran away and locked herself in my room to hide. I have told her millions of times to go hide in her own damn room!

I tried to scream but couldn't take it anymore; the air was so toxic and my head began to spin.

Next thing I knew I was falling, falling, and falling. Was I supposed to hit the ground? I just kept falling into another stage of darkness.

When I finally "landed", or woke up, I was accompanied by a bunch of random people in my face and blue and red lights flashing everywhere. They said Lilly had mixed milk, soap, cornstarch, and eggs together and tried to bake it with SCOTCH BONNET chillies and burnt it all. It had then caused a severe chemical reaction; its stench had reeked up the whole house. Luckily, I was fine, and I'd only passed out from fear and the very mild intoxication of the fumes that I inhaled. When I checked my phone, I had 49 missed calls and 234 message notifications! Just great, I had missed my outing with my friends at the mall. ☹

Lilly didn't even get punished! I was so furious with that little brat and Mom and Dad. On the other hand, though, I guess there's no point punishing her since she never learns... ☺   To be honest, if Lilly was MY child I would call the local zoo and take her back where she belongs. After that night, I was NEVER EVER going to eat out of that stove again.

The next day, during our free period, the first thing I did was find my friends and I updated them on the previous night's drama and why I didn't make the trip to the mall. They had cool stories to tell about their outing too, but they all admitted that mine was the best and most dramatic (I think so too, LOL). Just thinking about it makes me feel breathless!

As we made our way to Keira's house later that afternoon, we spent time studying for a bunch of quizzes and upcoming tests. This week dragged on and on, full of nothing but studying. There was no escape and no room for procrastination or we'd have low grades. Just the stress of all the revision and work put me in such a mood; I was ticked off by every little thing and I had an aggravated attitude towards anything or anyone that was in my way...

Finally, Saturday came! The girls and I had saved up for more shopping plus a small dinner date to celebrate our hard work and efforts in our exams. Unfortunately, Brittany and her petty little friends tagged along too. ☹

Therefore, we had to meet up at Brittany's house (by the house I mean a four-story mansion). Keira seemed fairly composed and said if we allowed them to come along, we could find some common interests and maybe even become "frenemies" at least.

The only interests I think they have are gossiping, shopping, and sucking up to Brit.☺ However, I didn't want to be the grinch of the day so I agreed with everyone else.

Soon after, we were getting into a car driven by Brittany's chauffeur. Before we even got to step inside the mall Brittany, Maddie, and Eliza were taking embarrassing selfies already. I hate to say it, but they looked sooo stupid. They were wobbling everywhere pouting, whilst the rest of us stood awkwardly behind them waiting to continue.

We all just rolled our eyes and headed upstairs. I stared in awe at the expensive clothes that I will probably never be able to afford and wished money would suddenly appear so I could buy them all. Keira pointed, laughed, and said, "Welcome to another version of Brittany's summer closet; come on, let's GO!" There were clear purses, neon swimsuits, lace summer gowns, retro sunglasses, velvet bucket hats, fishnet swimwear, and much more!

This place was bigger than the whole of Barbie's closet put TOGETHER (no, I don't watch Barbie, my little sister does).

I would have loved to buy everything I touched, but I knew my bank account didn't have the facilities to make that happen. ☹

Laura (obviously) started getting peckish and we decided to get some food. As we ate, Brittany, Maddie, and Eliza kept making petty little comments about Laura under their breath that caught our attention. They were like, "It's like the first time you've had a proper meal," or, "You should have a gender reveal for your food baby next week."

I was so mad! I was like, *Sis! Has your brain taken laxatives because you're talking a hundred percent crap,* but I only said it in my head because I wasn't having a fight with her whack self. ☺

Keira gave them the 'you-better-stop-that-now-or-you'll-be-in-trouble' look and they stopped straight away. We moved to another table and, just as things couldn't get any worse, the drama unfolded.

CHAPTER 2
Petty Battles

"Ha, jerks! We're not rude, I just say what others don't have the guts to say!" she shrieked. One of Brittany's most famous and disgusting quotes. Keira had had enough; I could see her brown eyes lighting up with anger and her expression getting tenser by the minute. She pushed out her chair, marched right up to Brittany's face, and said, "I'm surprised you haven't choked on all the trash you talk, Brit! You and your friends need to go and have a nice day SOMEWHERE ELSE." Finally, someone had put Brittany in her place and had shut her up!

However, Brittany was only getting started too. She re-sprayed her big blonde locks, adjusted her lip gloss and flung her own chair out of her way. "You know, Keira, two can play this silly little game. You try to start a war and I will end it. Don't ever think you can come to this school, use all my advice, use me for popularity AND steal my spotlight!"

Keira scoffed, "What spotlight? The only kind of light I know that you have is the flashlight on your cheap little phone."

Brittany looked highly offended; the look on her face was priceless. I was so sick of Brittany and by now I had made my mind up that she's 10 times worse than Lilly... She just doesn't learn! Then I stood up myself and went up to give Brittany a good piece of my mind.

"Actually Brittany, three can play this game and GIRL you have more issues than the *SO* magazine! So please, go and fix yourself before you try to fix others because you clearly need some work doing with your problematic self."

Keira looked back at me, smiled, and nodded. At this point, we could all tell Brittany had run out of things to say. Keira looked her up and down then continued, "Looks like queen of the school has dried out, would you like some tap water?" We shrieked at her hilarious remark, almost falling onto the floor.

That was when Brittany had one of the most hysteric meltdowns in history. It was the funniest thing EVER. ☺

She got the attention of all the employees and passers-by with her noise. When she was done raving about her so-called spotlight, she moved on to Maddie and Eliza, pushing them and threatening to spread crazy rumours about them! We sat there in awe as two broad, muscular security guards grabbed her and escorted her out of the restaurant.

Laura, being the good friend that she is, decided to be very 'helpful' by taking out her mobile phone and recording the whole incident. If the video leaked then it could possibly go viral; Brittany's dream is to be famous so I'm sure she'll be satisfied.☺

"Watch your back, Laura, I'll get you worse than you got me!" screamed Brittany just as she got dragged around the corner and out of sight. We rolled our eyes and imitated her childishly.

As we were heading home that evening, just as I expected, the video got leaked and it wasn't entirely viral yet, but it had about 14K views. We watched the video on repeat, laughing until we almost felt sick.

When we got back, Brittany was receiving a scolding from her maid and we were unable to go upstairs until she was done with her. It wasn't a really sensible idea, but we decided to carry on watching the video downstairs, since we just couldn't get over it.

When we were permitted to go upstairs, we snacked in Keira's room. As I was eating my crackers, I had a feeling that someone was watching me and felt the need to look behind. When I did so, Brittany was standing in the doorway staring straight at me. I made eye contact with her and quickly turned back around, ignoring her.

About 10 minutes later, my mild paranoia made me double-check over my shoulder again... There she was.

She just stood in the corner and glared at me. That was when I knew it was time for me to excuse myself and head home before it got dark. Apart from the drama, I enjoyed my day and I wanted to stay, but the scene I encountered with Brittany made me uncomfortable and I didn't want to stay longer to witness any of her wild payback stunts. I said my goodbyes, grabbed another cracker, and dashed out the gates.

I ran all the way home, locked the doors, and dropped on the floor in exhaustion, I was terrified that at some point on my run home I would look behind and see Brittany chasing after me. Luckily, nothing like that happened and I got home safely.

Sunday was a chill day for me, especially as Lewis' party was coming up in just two days; things were smooth. I decided to get ready and think about everything that could go wrong and then try to figure out a solution for it. Hey, I mean anything could go wrong, you never know ☺.

After thinking about everything bad that could possibly happen at the party, I tried on all three of the bathing suits I had picked out in the mall. I didn't want anything too skimpy and revealing—in case I had to suffer a severe wardrobe malfunction (I've seen celebs in the same situation and it didn't look fun). I also didn't want something too covering ... because I didn't want to look like some scuba diver or five-year-old girl. I also didn't want anything plain because I wanted to stand out. However, I didn't want to stand out too much!

When it comes to clothing hauls with me, it could take days to decide what I want.

After a while of trying on stuff and taking it back off, I finally decided to go with a neon bikini with a black, meshed beach gown on top; OMG, I loved it! I looked super cute in it (despite my chubby stomach).

I sent my friends a photo of myself for their opinions and they excitedly replied straight away, with great responses. ☺

Anyway, on top of the fact that my outfit looked bomb, I had spent the entire past few weeks trying to eat healthier and participate extra hard in gym classes, yet I STILL had the same jiggly potbelly as always. All that hard work and exhaustion wasn't even worth it. Now I wish I could've just lain at home eating chips, either way I still had the same stomach size. ☹

I decided to get some sleep. I also really wanted to give myself a DIY facial, but whenever I do try one, it does the opposite of what it's supposed to do.

I scrapped that idea. I remember once, when I had to attend my big sister's wedding, I tried one of those facials the night before; it turned out to be a terrible flop! Let's just say that after that event I became known as "the green-faced bridesmaid" in my family. Seriously, I don't know if these recipes are just a scam or if I'm just a clueless frog when it comes to skincare.

Well, that ends there and I'll just leave my face problem with the beauticians at the beauty parlour in the mall next time.

On Monday, I was so excited and I definitely wasn't the only one,

Everywhere I went everyone was talking about Lewis' Valentine's party!

I really felt that I had to make a good impression since loads of the popular kids were also attending, and my crush would be there too.

My BSFs agreed with me and thought the same. However, at free period Keira and Chloe reminded us that, as much as we wanted to make a good impression, we still had to be ourselves and not change for anyone or anything. If we did put on a fake personality, things would get messy. I totally agreed, but we still practised being calm and, instead of participating in swimming class, we stayed on the side and practised looking good coming in and out of the water.

We nailed it with the help of Keira; she looked like a real ocean goddess. She'd tell us stories about how it was like back

in Barcelona; sunshine, beaches, the fascinating sea, their food, and much more!

Also, our group of friends ended up getting a grade C on our overall skill scores of the sessions from the past few weeks...

I knew Mom and Dad were so going to ground me when they found out, but it was totally worth it because I was prepared for Lewis' party. ☺

After school that day, I was so excited and I wanted the day to end quickly, so I went straight to bed. Mom and Dad thought that I was being a bit suspicious, but I was just excited about the party ☺. The plan was to meet up at Brittany's house (yes, you must think that we're mad and absolutely not in our right senses, but that's where Keira was staying at the time while her parents were looking for a good house).

A chauffeur was responsible for taking us to the party, which was at Lewis' house—since his parents were away for the weekend.

I was so hyped up that I couldn't sleep properly that night. Even though I made a real effort to sleep early, I tossed and turned, only finally drifting off at midnight. I ended up looking like a tired scruffy rag ball in the morning. I brushed my teeth, jumped in the shower and out again, grabbed some fruit, and then ran out of the door (like I did on most weekdays).

"Hello, morning face!" Keira teased when she saw me. I was greeted by warm hugs and laughter from everyone. Life seemed perfect in that moment and I felt nostalgia for elementary school (the best years of my life so far). I wanted time to freeze and the moment to last forever. The sound of laughter and bubbly people filled my ears; the smell of warm buttered toast drifted up my nose; the feeling of safeness and enjoyment eased me, and I just wanted life to stay that way. I was living a real-life dream and things didn't stop there.

As I was embracing the current moment, Blake walked up to me smiling as his hazel eyes glistened with excitement under the bright rays of sunshine.

"Hey Kasey!" he began.

"Err, hi Blake!" I replied awkwardly, in case I said anything wrong.

"I was wondering ... since Lewis' Valentine's party is soon, well, like tomorrow, would you like to come with me to the party?"

OMG! Did Blake, just ask me out? I was about to die on the spot, I never EVER thought I would encounter a situation like this in my life. It was literally like a scene from those high school movies!

I smiled back and was about to scream yes but then remembered I planned to go with my BFFs and I did NOT want to betray them for the second time. I turned around and nervously glanced at my friends, who had been eagerly eavesdropping on our conversation the whole time! They all nodded in agreement and Alisha whisper-shouted, "Say yes, Kasey!"

"It's fine if you don't want to come with me, I totally understand," said Blake.

"No, No, I mean yes! I would love to come, thanks for the offer it would be amazing—no, I mean cool!" I blushed profusely and stood there like a naïve little girl who was dumbstruck by my crush fever.

"That's good; I'll pick you up at 10:30 a.m. tomorrow. See you." Then he was gone with the sun and nowhere to be seen.

I turned back to my friends and said, "I'm so sorry, guys, I just had to say—"

"YOU GO, GIRL, WHOO!" Laura interrupted.

"Oh my gosh, Blake just really asked you out!" Chloe cooed. They all laughed and hugged me. At that moment I felt so relieved and blessed.

Suddenly, we were rudely interrupted. Not by Brittany but by the school bell for registration! "Ugh." We sighed and trudged inside.☹

The day dragged on sooo slowly; nothing bad happened for once, but if I could describe my day it would be a "huge, fuzzy-blur of slowness."

I wasn't in the mood to do much or say much so I sat at the back of all my classes and drew in my sketch book. Thank goodness I was wearing my hoody because, if not, I would've been caught. I don't know what it is with the teachers in my school, but every time I sit at the back in my hoody, they seem to avoid me.

I wasn't complaining anyway because I really didn't want a teacher fussing all over me and purposely forcing me to answer questions when I didn't revise for them.

I was so relieved when the last bell rang to dismiss us from school.

Seriously, we're meant to only spend six hours in school (which, first of all, is way too long if you ask me), but today it seemed like I just sat there and did nothing but doodle and sketch for two weeks straight! As soon as that bell rang, my BFFs and I ran out of that place like wild animals.

That night, I 'borrowed' some of Mom's makeup and put my wild, dry locks in curlers. Then I went straight into bed. Luckily, this time, despite all the excitement and nerves I was experiencing, I fell asleep easier and faster.

CHAPTER 3
The Valentine's Party

As soon as I woke up, I showered and put all my makeup on. To be honest, I really don't have that much self-esteem, but I had to admit, I looked amazing!

FACE
MASK
FACE
MASK

After I finished washing and putting on my bikini, I only just realised that I had nothing to wear on top of it (excluding the beach gown). This was a total, utter DISASTER!

I had 30 minutes until Blake came to pick me up and I had been so excited in the past few days about making a good impression and picking a bikini that I had forgotten to pick out something to wear on top!

I couldn't get anything from my closet because everything in there was old and covered in fluff balls. I was so embarrassed; I started to have a little panic attack. Mom was trying to help, diving frantically in and out of her closet.

I highly doubted that she would have anything I would like in her closet, or at least something that suited me. I was done for, doomed, FINISHED! I was about to go back to my room, slam the door and start crying when...

Blake rang the bell AND Mom pulled out this gorgeous neon green-and-white sports jacket with matching track pants and shades.

They. Looked. Awesome! I never knew Mom would own something like that in her lifetime. I was in love with the fit and the fact that it complemented my curls just topped it off! ☺

I was so relieved and comforted, I felt like a million tonnes had been lifted off my shoulders. "Mom! Where did you find that?" I asked in awe.

"Oh, it's just one of my old tracksuits that I never wore back from when I studied in France," she said.

I slipped it on and gave my mom the biggest hug ever. Hey! She might not completely have the same style as me, but she sure knows how to mix and match colors and clothing.

Blake rang the bell again. Oops! I totally forgot he was there; I must've kept him waiting.

I ran downstairs, said my goodbyes to Mom and Dad then headed out the door.

"What's up, Kasey? It's so good to see you!" Blake said.

OH my gosh, I nearly fainted on the spot; Blake was at my front door talking to me! I was lost for words for a few seconds; then I regained my senses and stuttered, "OMG, hi Blake, I'm fantastic, I mean I'm good thanks. And you look amazing—sorry, I mean you look good. How are you?"

"I'm just excited for the party," he replied. "You look great too. I love the clothes you chose! Let's go."

Are you seriously telling me that this guy just said I looked great! I was suffering from a very severe "crush-en-gitis attack", but it was a very good attack ☺. I was so nervous throughout the whole ride; I kept texting my friends to update them on almost everything that happened. As we spoke, he moved his dirt-blond hair out of his face and his dark eyes locked on mine. OMG! I squirmed inside. If I had a dollar for every time I blushed during the ride, I would be the next teen millionaire. ☺

When we did arrive (about 25 minutes later), we joined everyone else in the photo booth queue to get our photos taken. Blake and I got nominated as the "cutest couple"—I couldn't believe it! ☺

We were having the time of our lives, whereas Brittany didn't seem to be enjoying the party at all. Her meltdown video from earlier was a trending topic in most conversations and, by now, everyone had seen her video. She sat in the corner of the garden embarrassed until Keira went over, pulled her up and began to dance with her. It looked hilarious at first; Brit wasn't having it, but eventually she looked somewhat happier.

Don't get me wrong, I despise Brittany and probably always will, but it made me smile to see her happy without causing some kind of drama. ☺

Overall, the pool was such fun and all that practicing that we did during swimming class paid off. Most of the time, we were goofing around, jumping on the huge pool floaties. I remember we were playing truth or dare, and Laura got dared to back flip off the diving board into the pool! She failed and instead body-planted right into the pool. As her body smacked against the surface of the water everyone went, "Oooohhh!" I got the video on my phone just in time and she burst out laughing. I loved the party and I was so glad it was drama-free. Anyways, I have a huge surprise that I've been hiding from you guys and I'm super excited. I'll write tomorrow. For now, goodnight! ☺

CHAPTER 4
España Aquí Vengo

OH MY GOSH! I actually don't even know where to start this CRAZY story; it's so hectic that when I think of it, I have a headache.

Well, to make things simple... We're on a family vacation for Lilly's seventh birthday (yes, today)! Now, let me just tell you, as soon as we got onto the plane I could smell a pungent mix of trouble, disaster, and disappointment coming our way.

WHY? It's Lilly, she's ruined EVERY vacation we've ever had! ☹

I know that you think I'm starting off very negative for a fun-sounding vacation. However, NEGATIVE is the correct word to describe how I was feeling as:

1. When we landed in Spain, my stomach felt so queasy and the heat was so thick and humid that I could feel and smell it on my face

2. The airport was filled with bustling people running everywhere!

3. Mom and Dad were arguing (as usual)

4. Since this was for Lilly's birthday, my big sister Tillie, her three kids, AND her fiancé came along too (as if there wasn't already enough of us to handle in a foreign country)

5. None of this was helping my frail and weak condition. Hey, come on, I could have passed out any second! (Okay maybe I'm overreacting, but HEY, it could have happened, you never know!)

Mom and Tillie had packed so much luggage full of unnecessary things we could do without. That meant more bags to carry! Nobody took into consideration that I felt terribly sick and at one point I almost got lost in the crowd. Luckily for Lilly, she had a kid lead, so she didn't have to take any responsibility for anything, let alone bother about getting lost.

Finally, we got to the minivan and I felt relieved to sit down in a cool, shaded, and comfy place. I lay my head on Tilly's shoulder as the suitcases were being loaded into the back of the car. I must've drifted off because, when I woke up again, we were outside what looked like a Spanish restaurant. Dad said we were stopping to eat. I checked my phone and it was 4:00 a.m. We had seriously stopped to eat in the middle of nowhere at this time ... wow!

We all sat around a little table outside in the dark, the only lights were the little colourful ones hanging around the streets. There were Spanish locals smoking, drinking, eating, and shouting all over. I found it funny, but Mom was displeased and told us not to look, although I do admit I couldn't stop glancing back.

We were foreigners and couldn't speak Spanish, so Tillie's fiancé did all the ordering for us. He's Venezuelan and can speak the language fluently. We dug into our grilled chicken and salad and fries then got back on the road again. As we got inside the car, I waved to the women and men that Mom had told me not to pay attention to; Lilly and the twins joined in too.☺

I knew Mom wanted to say something, but she kept it in because she didn't want to scold us on the first day of our vacation.

When we arrived at our villa, it was way past five in the morning and, by then, we were all so physically and mentally exhausted that we claimed a room, dumped our bags, found the nearest bed, fell on it and slept.

***

Today, I was so excited that I woke up at 8:00 a.m. and woke up all the kids in the villa. Our parents were still asleep, so we decided to quietly get ready for the day and check out the balcony.

The balcony was so high up, Lilly was scared (I found it hilarious), but of course we stayed away from the edges. I found some aloe vera plants and wild lilies growing nearby and copped them for myself.

We waited quite a while before the adults woke up, it was so boring and we had nothing to do!

1. I had no clue how to work the televisions round there

2. There was no food since this was a villa/apartment thing and we needed to get our own food

3. I didn't know the Wi-Fi password

4. The charging sockets here were totally different to the ones at home

So there we were, stuck doing nothing and waiting for about 35 more minutes for everyone else to wake up from sleep.

When they FINALLY did wake up, we let them know how long they'd left us awake with no food or Wi-Fi. Mom said we'd go and buy breakfast then start exploring. It was my job to look after my nieces, baby nephew, AND little sister whilst the grown-ups got their things ready and into the minivan. I wished my cousin Elsa was there, things would have been way more fun and she's an expert at dealing with kids (as you can see, I'm not good at dealing with children at all).

We headed straight over to this SuperCore market nearby to buy breakfast. We were only supposed to be getting breakfast, but we ended up going from shop to shop buying heaps of food.

Mom offered to help be the photographer for my Instagram and camerawoman for my YouTube vlog in return for keeping us out shopping for so long. I thought it was a great deal, so I quit complaining. ☺

We stayed out shopping for food so long that I already started to get a little tan ... and Lilly? That kid was sunburned LOL. She never listens and we all told her to put her sun cream on, but of course she didn't want to. ☹

When we got back after another hour or so from food shopping, we got to go in the pool!

I was so excited and of course so were Lilly and the twins. We all dived in straight away without even thinking how deep it would be! For the rest of the day we went from pool to pool, jumping, splashing around, and having fun. I felt like a little kid!

We had much fun that by the end of the day we were covered in mosquito bites and had a deep tan coming in already.

Oouch!

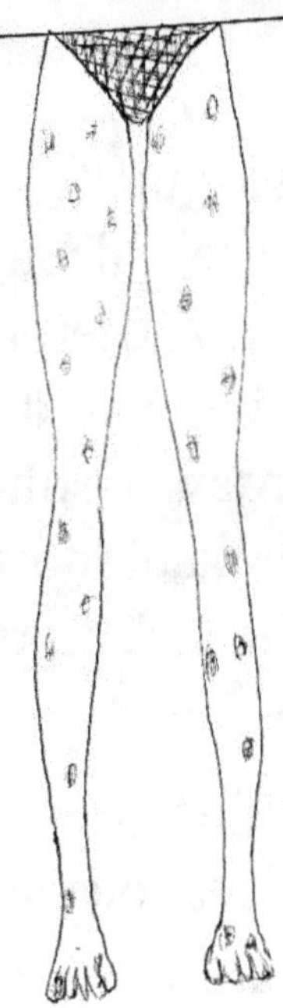

I had a great time and I really enjoyed the first day (I'm so glad there hasn't been any drama yet). Anyway, that's enough writing for today, my hands hurt! Ugh... One of my mosquito bites is bothering me! Goodnight, LOL. ☺

***

Today went so quickly. We all had breakfast out on the balcony in the hot sun and it was great! After breakfast, we tried out some new pools that we didn't get to visit yesterday. I sunbathed with Tillie and baby Raphael most of the time instead, leaving the girls in the pool with Tillie's fiancé.

Later this evening, we took a family stroll along some local beach.

The sun was setting, and the sky was a beautiful ombre of orange and pink; I could hear the waves crashing against the rocks and the aroma of Mediterranean Sea salt filled my nose. There were very few people there at the time and we found a small food hut nearby that was selling cold refreshments. We went over and Dad allowed us to get something each. A few moments later, I was sitting on the warm sand with my iceblast drink. We got going again after it was getting dark.

I couldn't wait to get back to the villa, by now the minivan was so cramped and humid. It almost made me feel trapped. I sat in the middle row in between Eva and Ava, who were screaming songs along with Lilly behind me.

Once we got back, I jumped out of that van immediately. I was soooo happy to be back again.

I went to the kitchen, grabbed a late-night snack and headed back to my room to write in my diary before going to bed. I thought of all my friends and Blake back at home. I wondered what they were doing. Were they thinking about me? Were they going out together? I wondered until I eventually nodded off.

***

Today, we woke up early and planned to go to Cabopino Beach (another nearby beach).

I so wanted to go, but then I also dreaded the minivan ride, so it took my parents a while to convince me to go; even though I complained and almost even cried a little I finally gave in and accepted.

It was a bright and hot day, just like any other day in Spain. The sun was roasting my skin and sand was burning my feet, but I loved it all the same. ☼ I sat in the shade vlogging on my phone with Tillie and Grayson (her fiancé).

Mom and Dad took Lilly and the twins out to the sea to catch some waves. When I finished vlogging a clip for my YouTube, I decided to go and join the other half of the family and catch some waves too.

To be honest, it was fun! ☺ I started on some small waves at first and once I adapted, I went on to tackling the big waves. We jumped over them and dived under them.

Eva, Ava, and Lilly got tired of the waves and ran off somewhere, with Mom and Dad chasing after them. Minutes after, Eva came back beckoning me to follow her.

I followed her across the boiling sand until we reached the others standing around a pile of sand. "Kasey, Kasey, look!" Ava squealed, pointing to the sand.

Lilly chipped in saying, "We made a sandcastle for any mermaids that get lost on shore and need a home."

I tilted my head sideways, examining the so-called "mermaid castle" and accidentally let out a laugh. I covered my mouth quickly in case they got upset, but it was too late. All three of them glared at me as if I'd just knocked down their pile of sand or something. Luckily, I was saved by Mom and, before things escalated, she called us over to a shaded spot to eat lunch.

Mom set out a picnic blanket with all sorts of exotic fruits, Spanish meats and delicious pastries we'd bought from the SuperCore market earlier. The way she set it out was so beautiful and symmetrical that I almost didn't want to ruin it, but I was hungry so...

I made sure to take as many videos and pictures of the food as I could for my social media feeds and just for memories in general. Once that was over with, we all tucked in. The food tasted just as good as it looked! So good we all went for seconds. I would've gone for a third round, but there wasn't enough left since there were ten of us in total. ☹

We went back to the sea and splashed around some more, cleaned ourselves in the showers and headed back once again.

Even though we were still in our bathing suits, we didn't like the idea of the showers at the beach being open and everyone being able to watch you showering, especially since all of the people there were strangers.

I even saw a lizard on the shower pole, which is kinda freaky for a city girl who doesn't like reptiles.

Anyway, I have to say that so far on this vacation, today was my favorite day. The minivan ride wasn't bad, I loved catching the waves, Mom's picnic was delicious, I got good content for all my social media and I enjoyed running around in the hot, grainy sand. What surprised me the most about today was that nothing went wrong, AT ALL! I expected Lilly or one of the twins to do something rebellious or Mom and Dad to have a silly argument, but NO. None of that happened! ☺

Of course I was happy, but it was so strange having an almost perfect day in my family that I almost even wanted something to go wrong to feel normal.

After a great dinner, we said our evening prayers and went straight to bed.

Usually, on vacation us kids always go to sleep late (or whenever we want), but with all the activities and things we'd done, our energy had waned and we felt the need to sleep straight away.

***

Today was the second to last day and it was SOOOO hectic. Why? Because it was "princess" Lilly's birthday and she was going to be seven and it was SUCH a big deal, so Mom and Dad made it seem like the whole world had to withdraw from their own lives and revolve around Lilly for the whole day.

I know I sound jealous, but I mean
who wouldn't be? Lilly gets special

treatment 24/7 anyway and today she was just getting quadruple the amount of attention she receives usually.

She could honestly have got away with murder at this point because it was her birthday. Nevertheless, as I am her sister I still (somehow) love her and must be grateful that I have a sister to begin with. At least that's what my parents say.

We were all forced to wake up 35 minutes earlier to decorate the place and go and wake Lilly up with a "Happy Birthday" song with breakfast in bed. LUCKY! We began to pack our bags early for tomorrow (our leaving day). Then we scrambled inside the minivan and went down south to one of the biggest shopping malls in Spain! We had to get Lilly's cake, bathing suit, party dress, more presents, new shades and a bunch of other things that weren't even necessary. It was such a tiring two hours and, as always, I was put in charge of supervising Eva, Ava, and Raphael with some help from Grayson.

Nothing satisfies me more than shopping, I love it! The difference this time is Mom and Dad were literally ignoring me. It was as if Tillie, Mom, and Dad were brainwashed. Lilly led the way screaming with glee and pointing at things. Whatever she pointed at it was all hers in two seconds.

And get this! We were continuing Lilly's shopping spree when we walked past a doughnut place that caught my attention. The aroma of the sweet delicacies made my mouth water and the bright colors of the toppings made my stomach yearn for them.

I asked Mom if she could get me ONE Oreo-flavored doughnut and this is exactly what she said to me: "Kasey, as you can tell, we don't have the money for that right now." Then she continued obsessing over my little sister.

Okay, but THAT just triggered my whole system on a different level! Like seriously, NOT ENOUGH MONEY? Oh please, I'm pretty sure if I collect all the receipts and count all the money spent on Lilly today it at least adds up to almost 5000 euros. That was when I decided to ditch them and walk around some stores by myself.

When I asked Mom if I could walk around by myself instead, she said, "Sure! Just call us if you need anything and stay safe." I rolled my eyes so hard that they could have popped out of their sockets and onto the floor.

Like seriously? Call us if you need anything? I JUST asked for something I needed, and you refused! Like is it just me, or are parents these days so confusing? If you agree (I'm sure most of you will) then write down something that your parents have said/done that confused you.

Anyway, after that I continued walking around the mall snacking on sample foods because I was so hungry and my parents "couldn't possibly afford" to buy me food, despite spending almost 5000 euros on my little sister. ☹

Yup, I get it, completely understandable! I really didn't know what else to think or do at this point, so I went to Grayson to see if he could help me out. Lucky for me, he handed me 17 euros. I know it wasn't as much as 5000, but it was enough to get me not just one but a whole box of those doughnuts I had been looking forward to buying.☺

After what seemed like an eternity, we were out the mall and off for Lilly's birthday lunch at a restaurant by the beach we visited yesterday. I was happy to hear that because, as always, I was still hungry. I had chosen to wear a short black dress and I hadn't thought until now that it wasn't a good idea. The sun was boiling me like a pot of soup. I was happy to get inside the restaurant and out of the sun for a while.

We were served a huge portion of paella mariscos (a Spanish dish) with hot, buttered baguettes for appetisers. It tasted so good that I ate my mom's too, but I quickly stopped myself after I had a sudden flashback to the "bacon balm" story in my last diary. Long story short; I ate too many balms and nearly threw up all over the mall then I was unwell for a few days and didn't go to school.

Anyway, I didn't really eat that much except the prawns, shrimp, and rice. I didn't like the shellfish or the little yellow squidgy fish bits. For dessert, we had a "PJ Masks" birthday cake stuffed with ice cream and chocolate fillings. Oh, it was soooo GOOD! I knew what time it was next, it was that 45 minutes of awful cheesy smiling and posing for photos so that Mom could post them on her Facebook feed! We had to sing "Happy Birthday" to Lilly three times just for Mom's live video and we each had to say why we loved Lilly and what we wish for her in the future. Obviously, Lilly loved the attention and it didn't help that she wanted Mom and Dad to take more photos and videos. Once Mom's phone storage was full to the brim, she took Dad's phone and started making videos.

I excused myself and pretended to use the restroom because I knew what would happen next. Dad's storage would fill up; then I would have to hand over MY phone! ☹

NO WAY was I going to hand over my personal property to Mom just to have it filled with goofy photos of Lilly smiling with a bunch of missing teeth.

My mouth was so tired of smiling afterwards; I think my cheeks could have stretched a few inches wider. I was so glad to leave!

When we went on a speedboat ride afterwards to watch the amber sunset, I could barely even walk because of how full I was. Other than that, the setting was perfect; the waves glistened like crystals, my curly mad hair blew perfectly in the wind, the salty aroma of seawater filled my nostrils and the faint sounds of laughter from Mom, Dad. and Lilly were ringing in my ears. I just wished I could have captured that moment forever....

This evening, I've spent some time writing in my diary on the balcony. I've studied the sky and the picturesque setting; it's been such a good ending to my vacation. After I put my pen down, I think I might just fall asleep. After all of this, I am so exhausted and I have a plane to catch home tomorrow. I love my family, but I'm too tired for any more family drama, I can't wait to tell all my BFFs about my vacation. Goodnight xxx ✈

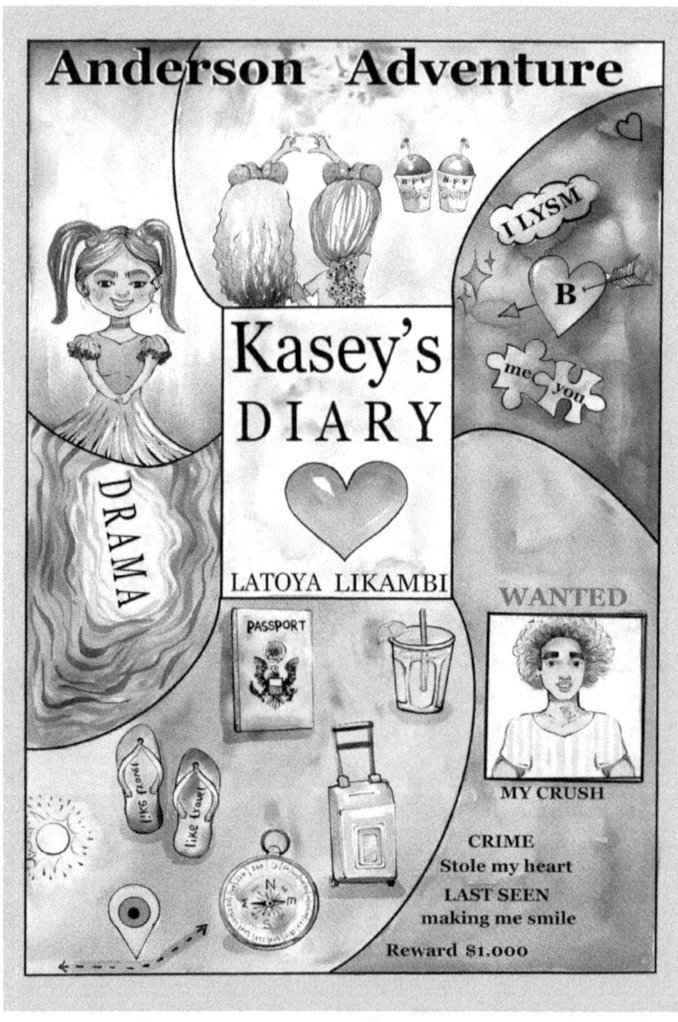
Anderson Adventure
I LYSM
B
me you
Kasey's
DIARY
LATOYA LIKAMBI
DRAMA
PASSPORT
like travel
like travel
N
WANTED
MY CRUSH
CRIME
Stole my heart
LAST SEEN
making me smile
Reward $1.000

the Anderson family!!!
Kasey's
DIARY
LATOYA LIKAMBI
POPULAR
LONDON
School
New Teacher

About The Author

Latoya Likambi is Liverpool's youngest best-selling author, an entrepreneur, and a positive role model for children globally. She is a highly confident, eloquent, and inspiring young speaker and influencer, with a passion to inspire young people to unleash their creative genius and fulfill their maximum potential, while staying authentic and true to themselves. She has featured on diverse national and international Radio and TV stations, and has been a guest speaker in various schools, community groups, business events/ conferences, and in The House of Commons.

She is the founder of Teyes Eye Skincare & Cosmetics and co-founder/ mentor at Likambi Global Publishing.

Latoya is highly inspired by her mum, Dr. Sylvia Forchap-Likambi, Jacqueline Wilson, and Rachel Renee Russell; and hopes to write a series of books that will be available to read in schools across the country and abroad.

You can find out more about her work and her books at Likambi Global Publishing.

"You can still be confident even if you are bullied. You shouldn't listen to what bullies say about you… and you must understand that they often have problems they are struggling with – somewhere."

Latoya Likambi

Website:

www.likambiglobalpublishing.com

Email:

enquiries@likambiglobalpublishing.com

Address:

208a Picton Road, Liverpool, L15 4LL

United Kingdom

www.ingramcontent.com/pod-product-compliance
Lightning Source LLC
Chambersburg PA
CBHW070506170726
48291CB00008B/2680